9P/J
X

# MARKO THE RICH
# AND
# VASILY THE UNLUCKY

# MARKO THE RICH
# AND
# VASILY THE UNLUCKY

Translated from the Russian by
## THOMAS P. WHITNEY
## Illustrated by IGOR GALANIN

MACMILLAN PUBLISHING CO., INC.
**New York**
COLLIER MACMILLAN PUBLISHERS
London

The illustrations are full-color tempera paintings. The typeface is Aster, with the display set in Abbot Old Style.

*Marko the Rich and Vasily the Unlucky* is translated from the Afanasyev collection of Russian folk tales.

Library of Congress Cataloging in Publication Data     Main entry under title: Marko the rich and Vasily the unlucky.     "Translated from the Afanasyev collection of Russian folk tales."     [1. Folklore—Russia]  I. Whitney, Thomas P., tr. II. Galanin, I., illus.     PZ8.1.M33     398.2'2'0947     [E]     73-6043     ISBN 0-02-792710-5

**TO THE MASSIE FAMILY**
**—I.G.**

In a certain kingdom there once lived a very rich merchant. He had an only child, a small daughter called Anastasiya the Beautiful.

The merchant was named Marko, and was known to everyone as Marko the Rich. Marko could not stand the poor, and his servants had orders to set the dogs on any beggars that stopped at his house.

One day Marko saw two ancient, gray-haired men standing beneath his window, and ordered the dogs to be unleashed on them. But Anastasiya the Beautiful heard him and pleaded with her father:

"Dear Father! If only for my sake, please let them spend the night in the stables." And her father agreed. When everyone in the house had gone to sleep Anastasiya crept out of bed and went to the stables. She climbed up the log wall of the shed in which the men slept, and stood watching them.

The time came for matins. At the stable icon the lighted candle seemed to grow brighter. The old men arose, took priests' robes out of their packs, and after putting the robes on, began to pray.

An angel of God flew down to them and spoke: "My Lords! In the village over the mountain, a son has been born in the family of a peasant. What name shall he be given, and what is the fate you have in store for him?"

One of the old men replied: "I name him Vasily the Unlucky, and bless him with all the wealth of Marko the Rich in whose stable we have spent this night."

Anastasiya heard these words and returned to the house. Dawn came, and the old men left. Anastasiya went to her father and told him everything that she had seen and heard in the stable.

Marko did not believe the words of the old man, but nevertheless he decided to see whether a boy had actually been born in the village mentioned. He ordered his carriage readied for a

journey and traveled to the village, where he went directly to the priest:

"Was there a boy born in your village on such and such a night?"

"Yes!" said the priest. "On that night a boy was born to the poorest peasant in the village. I myself named him Vasily the Unlucky. But I have not yet christened him because I have found no one willing to be the child's godparent."

Marko said he would be the child's godfather and gave instructions that a fine feast be prepared for the christening. The infant was brought, christened, and feasted to everyone's satisfaction.

The next day Marko the Rich sent for the poor peasant.

"Friend! Father of my godchild!" Marko said. "You are a very poor man and will not be able to bring up your son with the best advantages. Give him to me. I will see to it that he is educated and becomes a person of substance. And in the meantime I will give you a thousand rubles."

The old man thought and thought and finally agreed. Marko gave the promised money to the peasant, took the child, wrapped him in robes of fox fur because it was wintertime, put him in the carriage, and drove off.

After they had traveled several miles they passed a ravine. Marko the Rich ordered the carriage stopped. He gave his godson to his servant and said:

"Take him by the feet and throw him into that ravine!" The servant did as he had been ordered. As the carriage started on its way, Marko shouted, "Now let me see you take all I possess!"

The following day it happened that some merchants were traveling along the same road Marko had taken. They were bringing Marko twelve thousand rubles with which to repay a debt they owed him. When they came to the ravine into which the baby had been thrown, they heard a child's cry. They stopped and sent a servant to see what it was. The servant climbed down into the ravine, and found a baby lying in a field of flowers. The servant could not believe what he saw. He called to the merchants, who came to see for themselves. They carried the child to the carriage, wrapped him in furs, and rode off.

They arrived at Marko's house, and when they told him how they had found the child, Marko knew at once that it was his godson.

He asked Anastasiya to take care of the baby while he entertained the merchants. He gave them liquor and wine and asked them to turn the boy over to him. At first the merchants would not agree, but finally, when Marko offered to forgive their entire debt, they gave him the child and rode away.

Anastasiya immediately found a cradle, hung it with curtains, and looked after the little boy—never leaving him day or night. One day passed, and another. On the third day Marko returned home rather late. Anastasiya was sleeping, and he stole the infant out of the cradle. Marko put him in a barrel, tarred the barrel, and threw it off the wharf into the sea.

The little barrel floated on and on until it floated by a monastery. At that very moment a monk had come to fetch water. He heard a child's cry which seemed to come from a floating barrel. He immediately got into a boat, fished the barrel out of the water, broke it open, found the child, and brought him to the abbot of the monastery. The abbot named the child Vasily the Unlucky, and from then on he lived in the monastery. In time he learned to read and write. The abbot loved him and made him warden of the monastery's treasure.

When Vasily was sixteen, it happened that Marko the Rich stopped at the monastery. He had been traveling for a year collecting debts. Marko was accorded the honors reserved for a man of wealth. The abbot ordered the warden to light candles in the church, and to sing and read the liturgy. Marko the Rich asked the abbot how long the boy had been at the monastery.

The abbot related how, when a baby, the boy had been rescued from a barrel floating in the sea. When the abbot mentioned how many years ago it had been, Marko soon realized that the young warden was his godson, and so he said to the abbot:

"If only I had such an efficient chap as your warden working for me, I would make him my chief steward and entrust my entire fortune to him for safekeeping. Would you not free him to work for me?"

The abbot hesitated a long time. But when Marko offered to give the monastery twenty-five thousand rubles in exchange for

the warden, the abbot decided to take up the matter with the other monks. They considered what to do, and finally agreed to release Vasily the Unlucky so that he might go with Marko.

Marko continued on his travels, but he sent Vasily home with a letter which the young man was to deliver to Marko's wife. The letter said:

"Wife: As soon as you receive my letter, take the bearer to the soap factory, and as you pass the great cauldron, push him into it. See to it that these instructions are carried out! If you do not do as I have written, you shall pay for it! This young fellow is my enemy!"

Vasily took the letter and started on his way to Marko's house. On the road he met an old man who stopped him and asked:

"Where are you going, Vasily the Unlucky?"

"To the home of Marko the Rich with a letter for his wife," Vasily replied.

"Show me the letter!"

Vasily took the letter out of his pocket and handed it to the old man, who broke its seal and gave it back to Vasily to read. Vasily read it and began to weep:

"What have I done to this man that he should want to have me killed?"

The old man comforted him: "Do not weep," he said, "for God will not abandon you!"

The old man blew upon the letter, and it was again sealed as it had been before he opened it. Then he said to Vasily:

"Continue on your journey and when you arrive, give the letter to Marko's wife."

And Vasily did so. Marko's wife read the letter, considered the matter, summoned her daughter Anastasiya and read it to her. The letter said:

"Wife: The very next day after you receive this letter, marry Anastasiya to the bearer. Do so without fail! If you do not, you will answer to me!"

Among the wealthy everything is always ready—wine, food, everything needed for a feast or even a wedding. Vasily was dressed in fine clothing and presented to Anastasiya. She fell in love with him at once, and they were married.

One day Marko's wife was informed that the ship on which her husband was traveling was sailing in. With her son-in-law and daughter she went down to the wharf to meet it. When Marko saw his son-in-law, he flew into a rage:

"How did you dare marry our daughter to him?" he said to his wife.

"I followed your orders," she replied.

Marko demanded to see the letter he had sent her, but when he read it, he was forced to admit that the handwriting was his.

Marko did nothing for a month, for a second month, and for a third. Then one day he summoned his son-in-law:

"Here is a letter," he said. "You are to take it beyond the thrice-ninth land to the thrice-tenth kingdom, to my friend, King Zmei, the fire-breathing, smoke-eating, winged snake-dragon.

You must collect from him the twelve years' tribute that he owes me for building a palace on my land. And also find out what happened to my twelve sailing ships that have not been heard from in three years. And you must set off tomorrow morning!"

Vasily took the letter, went to his wife, and told her everything Marko the Rich had ordered him to do. Anastasiya wept bitterly, but she did not dare ask her father to change his mind.

Vasily left early the next morning, having prayed to God and filled his pouch with pieces of dried bread for the journey. He had traveled a long time, or perhaps it was not so long, when he heard a voice saying:

"Vasily the Unlucky, where are you going?"

He looked about him and saw no one. "Who is calling me?" he said.

"I, the oak tree, am asking where you are going," the voice replied.

"I am on my way to King Zmei to collect the twelve years' tribute he owes Marko the Rich."

And the oak replied: "When you see the king remind him that the oak has been standing for three hundred years; ask him if it still has a long time to stand."

Vasily said he would do so and went on his way.

He came to a river, where he boarded the ferry that took people across. The ferryman asked:

"Where are you going, my friend?"

Vasily told him, just as he had told the oak.

The ferryman asked Vasily to remind the king that he had been ferrying for thirty years, and was he to continue for a long time still?

"Very well," said Vasily, "I will do so!"

He continued on his way till he came to the sea. There, from shore to shore, lay a gigantic whale, and people were traveling back and forth on its back as if it were a bridge. As Vasily was walking across, the whale suddenly asked:

"Vasily the Unlucky, where are you going?"

Vasily repeated what he had told the oak tree and the ferryman—and the whale, too, had a request for the king.

"Will you remind the king that the whale has been lying across the sea for so long that the horses and people going back and forth have worn down its body to the bones? And will it have to lie there for a long time still?"

Vasily promised and went on. He came to a green meadow in the midst of which there stood a great palace. Vasily entered the palace, and as he walked through the rooms he noticed that each was more beautifully furnished and more luxurious than the one before it. When he came to the last room of all, he saw a beautiful maiden lying on a bed and weeping bitterly. As soon as she saw Vasily she arose, came toward him, and asked:

"Who are you, and why have you come to this accursed palace?"

Vasily showed her Marko's letter and explained that Marko

had sent him to collect from King Zmei the twelve years' tribute the king owed Marko.

The maiden took the letter and threw it into the fire. Then she said:

"Marko sent you here not to collect tribute from King Zmei but to be eaten by him. But tell me by what road you came here. Did you hear or see anything strange along the way?"

Vasily told her about the oak tree, the ferryman, and the whale.

He had hardly finished when the earth and the palace began to shake. The maiden immediately hid Vasily in a trunk, and as she closed the lid, said:

"Listen carefully to what Zmei and I talk about!"

As soon as King Zmei entered the room, he said:

"How is it that I smell the breath of a Russian?"

"How can you smell the breath of a Russian here?" the maiden replied. "You've been flying about Holy Russia all day and surely you've inhaled a lot of Russian air!"

"That's probably it," Zmei said. "I'm very tired. Sit by my side and pick the lice off my head!" And the King lay down on the bed.

"King, what a dream I had while you were away!" the maiden said. "I saw myself walking along a road, and an oak tree cried out to me: 'Ask your king how long I must still stand here!'"

And King Zmei replied: "The oak will stand there until someone comes up to it and pushes it from the east with his foot. Then the oak will topple over, roots and all, and beneath it will

be found such a mass of gold and silver as even Marko the Rich has never seen!"

"And then in my dream I came to a river, where the ferryman asked me how long he would still have to ferry people from shore to shore."

"If he allows the first person who comes along to get aboard, and then pushes the ferry off and remains behind himself, whoever it is will become the eternal ferryman, and he will be able to go home at last!"

"I also dreamed that I was walking across the sea on the back of a whale, and it asked me how long it must still lie there."

"It will lie there until it coughs up the twelve ships of Marko the Rich. When it does, it will be able to swim away, and its flesh will grow back again."

When he had finished speaking, King Zmei fell into a deep sleep.

The maiden let Vasily the Unlucky out of the trunk and said:

"Do not tell the whale what you have heard until you cross to the far side of the sea. Only then tell it to cough up the twelve ships of Marko the Rich. Do the same when you come to the ferryman. While you are on the near side do not tell him what you have heard, but wait until he has ferried you across. As for the oak tree, only if you push it from the east with your foot will it fall over and reveal to you the great treasure beneath."

Vasily the Unlucky thanked the maiden and left for home.

He came to the whale, and the whale said:

"Did you ask King Zmei?"

"I did. When I have crossed to the other side, I will tell you his answer."

And when he reached the far side, Vasily said to the whale:

"Cough up the twelve ships of Marko the Rich."

The whale did as it was told and the ships sailed off under full sail—totally unharmed. And as a result Vasily the Unlucky stood up to his knees in water.

Vasily came to the ferryman, and the ferryman asked:

"Did King Zmei speak of me?"

"He did," said Vasily. "Take me across and I will tell you what he said."

When they got to the other side of the river, Vasily said to the ferryman:

"Whoever comes to you first, let him board the ferry, push it from shore, and remain behind. That person will have to ferry people back and forth for all eternity, and you will be able to go home at last."

Vasily the Unlucky came to the oak tree and pushed it with his foot from the east, and the oak fell down. Beneath it Vasily found gold and silver and precious stones beyond belief!

Vasily looked back to the sea and saw that the twelve ships coughed up by the whale were sailing straight for the shore.

The lead ship was captained by the same old man whom

Vasily had met when he was on his way from Marko the Rich with the letter for Marko's wife.

The old man said to Vasily: "Here, Vasily, is what God has blessed you with!"

He turned the ships over to Vasily and went on his way. The sailors loaded the oak tree's treasure onto the ships, and when all was ready they set sail. Word was sent ahead to Marko the Rich that his son-in-law was on his way home with the twelve ships, and that King Zmei had rewarded Vasily with great wealth.

Marko became enraged that his plan had failed. He gave orders for his carriage to be brought, and he left for King Zmei's palace to reproach him.

He came to the ferry, and as soon as he had seated himself, the ferryman pushed the ferry from shore—and it was Marko the Rich who became the eternal ferryman.

As for Vasily the Unlucky, he returned home to his wife and his mother-in-law, and they all lived together happily. They helped the poor, gave food and drink to the needy, and Vasily the Unlucky was indeed blessed with all the wealth and possessions of Marko the Rich.